World of Reading

REY'S JOURNEY

WRITTEN BY ELLA PATRICK
ART BY BRIAN ROOD

LOS ANGELES · NEW YORK

For information address Disney • Lucasfilm Press, 1200 Grand Central Avenue, Glendale, California 91201.

Printed in the United States of America

First Edition, December 2017 10 9 8 7 6 5 4 3 2 1

Library of Congress Control Number on file

FAC-029261-17305

ISBN 978-1-4847-8183-8

Visit the official *Star Wars* website at: www.starwars.com.

Rey and Chewbacca raced through space in the *Millennium Falcon*.
Rey had a map that led them to a small planet.
The planet was called Ahch-To.

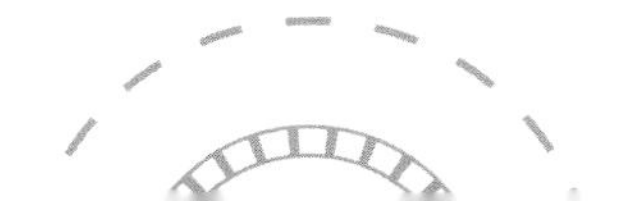

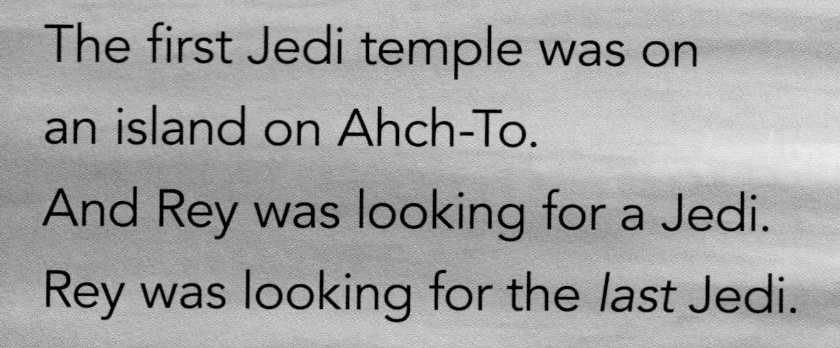

The first Jedi temple was on
an island on Ahch-To.
And Rey was looking for a Jedi.
Rey was looking for the *last* Jedi.

The island was very green.
Some strange creatures lived there.
Small birds called porgs
sat among the rocks.
And alien Caretakers
took care of the island.

But Luke Skywalker also lived there.
Luke Skywalker was the last Jedi.
Rey had finally found him!
Rey gave Luke his old lightsaber.
The Jedi used lightsabers
to protect the galaxy.

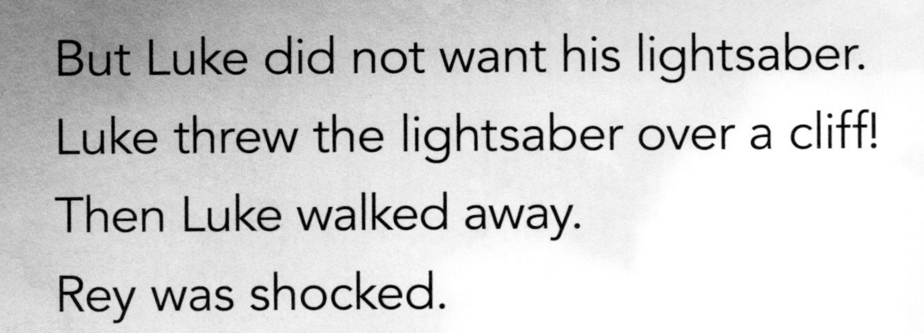

But Luke did not want his lightsaber.
Luke threw the lightsaber over a cliff!
Then Luke walked away.
Rey was shocked.

Rey went to find the lightsaber.
Then she saw Luke's old X-wing.
It was underwater.
Luke never wanted to leave the island.
Rey was confused.
Why would Luke not talk to her?

Luke would not talk to Rey.
But he *would* talk to Chewie.
Luke was surprised
to see his old friend.
Was his friend Han Solo there, too?

Rey told Luke how the evil
Kylo Ren had defeated Han Solo.
Kylo Ren was a First Order warrior.
Luke's sister, Leia,
led the Resistance that fought
against the First Order.

Across the galaxy, First Order ships attacked the Resistance fleet. Leia needed Luke's help to defeat Kylo Ren and the First Order.

But Luke would not leave the island.
He would not help the Resistance.

Rey would not give up.

Rey followed Luke every day.

She followed him across the island.

Luke fished and found other food.

But Luke never spoke to Rey.

He never even looked at her.

Then one day, as Rey followed Luke,
something called to her.
It was the Force.
The Force was an energy field
that connected all living things.
Rey walked away from Luke.

The Force led Rey to an old tree.
There were very old
Jedi books inside the tree.
The Force told Rey to touch the books.
Then Luke appeared.

Rey told Luke that
the Resistance needed him.
But Rey needed Luke, too.
Rey felt the Force inside of her.
But she did not know how to use it.

Rey needed a teacher.
But Luke did not want to teach Rey.
He had trained Kylo Ren to be a Jedi,
before Kylo joined the First Order.
Luke never wanted to teach
anyone ever again.

But Rey still would not give up.
She would follow Luke until
he agreed to teach her.
Rey would not leave Luke alone.

Meanwhile, the porgs would not leave Chewie alone.
Chewie was mad at first.
He roared at them!
But then he grew to like them.
Chewie and the porgs were friends.

While Chewie made new friends,
Luke found an old friend.
He went to the *Millennium Falcon*
and found R2-D2.
The droid beeped with happiness.
R2-D2 had missed Luke.

R2-D2 showed Luke an old hologram.
It was a message from long ago.
It was young Leia asking for help.
Luke had helped his sister then.
And she needed his help again.
Luke decided to train Rey.

Luke would teach Rey
the ways of the Jedi.

Rey would learn
the power of the Force.

Maybe Luke would not be the last Jedi after all. . . .